THIS WALKER BOOK BELONGS TO:

Jenny Mike Amelia Sophie

First published 1993 by
Walker Books Ltd
87 Vauxhall Walk
London SE11 5HJ

This edition published 1995

2 4 6 8 10 9 7 5 3

© 1993 Marcia Williams

This book has been typeset in Klang.

Printed in Hong Kong

British Library Cataloguing in Publication Data
A catalogue record for this book is
available from the British Library.

ISBN 0-7445-3625-1

Don Quixote

Retold and Illustrated by
Marcia Williams

WALKER BOOKS
AND SUBSIDIARIES
LONDON · BOSTON · SYDNEY

Now, to the eccentric Don Quixote the inn was a castle

and the innkeeper and travellers fine lords and ladies.

To them, Don Quixote was a madman, but they made him welcome

and the innkeeper agreed to dub him a "true" knight

if he could guard his armour until morning.

Putting his armour on a water trough, Quixote marched before it.

All went well until a carrier came to get water for his mules.

Furious at the disturbance, Don Quixote knocked the man unconscious

and moments later broke another carrier's head in four places.

The other travellers, woken by the noise, began to stone him.

challenged to declare his Dulcinea the fairest Lady in the world.

When they refused, Don Quixote raised his lance and charged;

but Rocinante fell and it was the knight who was sorely beaten.

But where Don Quixote saw giants, Sancho saw windmills!
As Quixote charged towards them, the wind rose and
when he struck the nearest sail it turned with such force that
his lance broke, flinging both horse and rider to the ground.

Sancho rushed to his master's aid, wondering how

a famous knight could mistake windmills for giants!

They spent that night under some trees and

the next day journeyed on, until they saw

two monks on the road, followed by a lady in a coach.

Battered and weary, Don Quixote and Sancho Panza

spent the night with a group of astonished goatherds,

riding on next morning until they reached a stream.

Rocinante wandered over to some grazing mares,

but the unfriendly animals kicked and bit him.

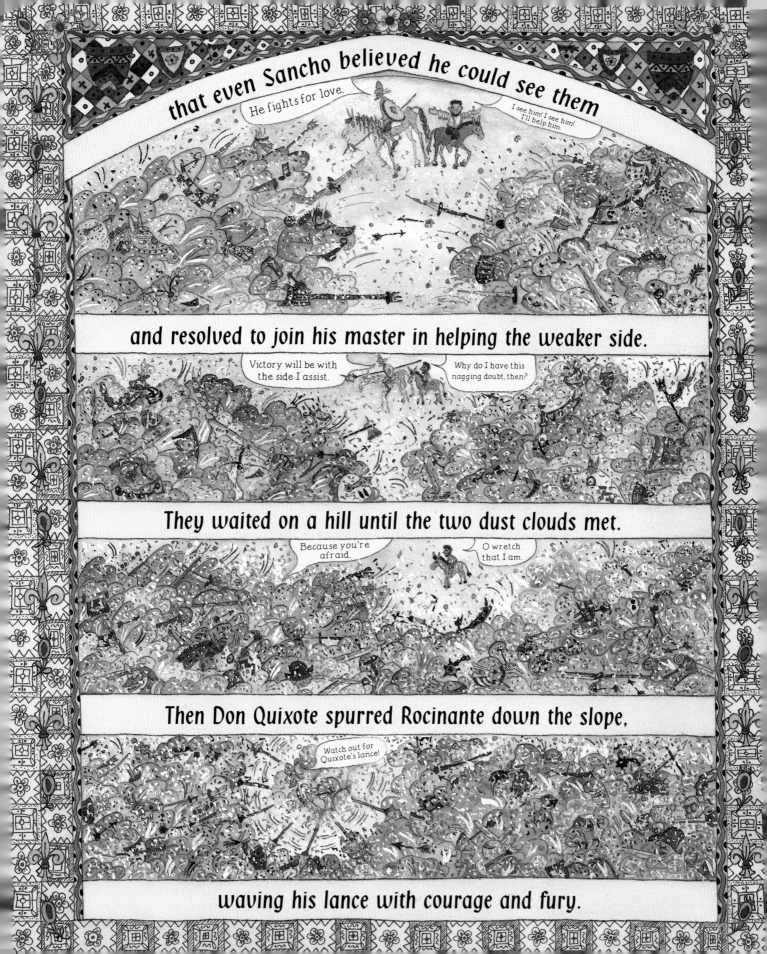

PORTUGAL

LA MANCHA